DATE DUE

The House that that Bob Built

ROBERT A.M. STERN
Illustrated by Andrew Zega

RIZZOLI
NEW YORK

First published in the United States of America in 1991 by
Rizzoli International Publications, Inc.
300 Park Avenue South, New York, New York 10010

Library of Congress Cataloging-in-Publication Data

Stern, Robert A. M.
    The house that Bob built / retold and illustrated by
Robert A.M. Stern.
        p.   cm.
    A retelling of The house that Jack built.
    Summary: Retells the cumulative rhyme "The house
that Jack built" to describe a pleasant and comfortable
house with an ocean view.
    ISBN 0-8478-1369-X
    (1. Dwellings—Fiction.   2. Stories in rhyme.)
I. House that Jack built.   II. Title.
PZ8.3.S8394Ho   1991
(E)—dc20   90-26901
                                                CIP
                                                AC

Typography by Graphic Arts Composition
Printed and bound by Tien Wah Press, Singapore

Design by Milton Glaser, Inc.

The House that Bob Built

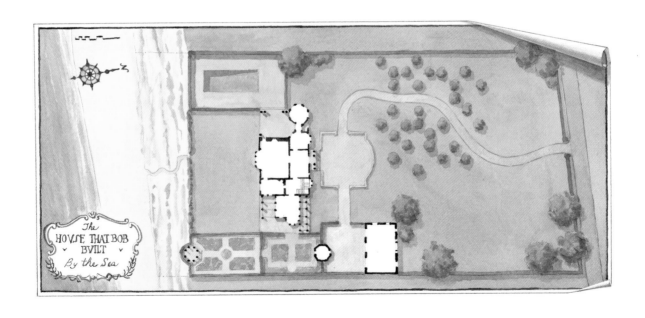

The
HOVSE THAT BOB
BVILT
By the Sea

*T*his is the door
at the front of the house that Bob built.

*T*his is the floor
that leads to the door
at the front of the house that Bob built.

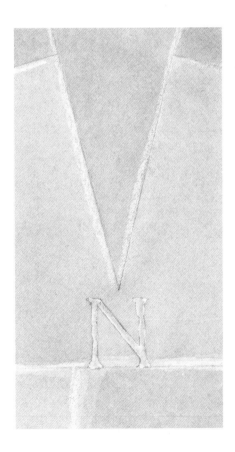

*T*his is the hall
that welcomes the guests
who cross the floor
that leads to the door
at the front of the house that Bob built.

*T*his is the parlor that faces the west
next to the hall that welcomes the guests
who cross the floor
that leads to the door
at the front of the house that Bob built.

*T*his is the porch for quiet and rest
outside the parlor that faces the west
next to the hall that welcomes the guests
who cross the floor
that leads to the door
at the front of the house that Bob built.

This is the garden misted with dew
beyond the porch for quiet and rest
outside the parlor that faces the west
next to the hall that welcomes the guests
who cross the floor
that leads to the door
at the front of the house that Bob built.

This is the library with an ocean view
across from the garden misted with dew
beyond the porch for quiet and rest
outside the parlor that faces the west
next to the hall that welcomes the guests
who cross the floor
that leads to the door
at the front of the house that Bob built.

*T*his is the room where eight can dine
next to the library with an ocean view
across from the garden misted with dew
beyond the porch for quiet and rest
outside the parlor that faces the west
next to the hall that welcomes the guests
who cross the floor
that leads to the door
at the front of the house that Bob built.

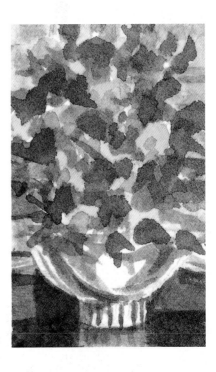

*T*hese are the stairs that let you climb
outside the room where eight can dine
next to the library with an ocean view
across from the garden misted with dew
beyond the porch for quiet and rest
outside the parlor that faces the west
next to the hall that welcomes the guests
who cross the floor
that leads to the door
at the front of the house that Bob built.

This is a bedroom all clean and bright
atop the stairs that let you climb
outside the room where eight can dine
next to the library with an ocean view
across from the garden misted with dew
beyond the porch for quiet and rest
outside the parlor that faces the west
next to the hall that welcomes the guests
who cross the floor
that leads to the door
at the front of the house that Bob built.

This is the study filled with light
beside the bedroom all clean and bright
atop the stairs that let you climb
outside the room where eight can dine
next to the library with an ocean view
across from the garden misted with dew
beyond the porch for quiet and rest
outside the parlor that faces the west
next to the hall that welcomes the guests
who cross the floor
that leads to the door
at the front of the house that Bob built.

This is the playroom under the eaves
near the study filled with light
beside the bedroom all clean and bright
atop the stairs that let you climb
outside the room where eight can dine
next to the library with an ocean view
across from the garden misted with dew
beyond the porch for quiet and rest
outside the parlor that faces the west
next to the hall that welcomes the guests
who cross the floor
that leads to the door
at the front of the house that Bob built.

*T*his is the weather vane
as high as the leaves
over the playroom under the eaves
near the study filled with light
beside the bedroom all clean and bright
atop the stairs that let you climb
outside the room where eight can dine
next to the library with an ocean view
across from the garden misted with dew
beyond the porch for quiet and rest
outside the parlor that faces the west
next to the hall that welcomes the guests
who cross the floor
that leads to the door
at the front of the house that Bob built.

*T*his is the house that Bob built.

ROBERT A.M. STERN *is an internationally recognized architect, teacher and writer, and founder and Senior Partner of Robert A.M. Stern Architects of New York City. During the last two decades, his firm has received numerous awards and honors for design excellence, including the National Honor Award of the American Institute of Architects in 1980, 1985, 1990 and 1991. Mr. Stern has long been a recognized leader in residential design, and this book is in many ways a summation and celebration of the firm's continuing work in the Shingle Style vernacular of the northeastern states.*

A Fellow of the American Institute of Architects, Mr. Stern is a Professor at the Graduate School of Architecture, Planning and Preservation at Columbia University, and was first director of Columbia's Temple Hoyne Buell Center for the Study of American Architecture. He is author of numerous books and articles on architecture, as well as the subject of many articles and monographs documenting his work. In 1986, he hosted "Pride of Place: Building the American Dream," an eight-part television documentary aired nationally on the Public Broadcasting System. Mr. Stern is a graduate of Columbia and Yale Universities, and lives in Manhattan.